Sports Alive!

Team Skydiving

by Charles and Linda George

Consultant:
Dany Brooks
Director of Communications
United States Parachute Association

RiverFront Books

an imprint of Franklin Watts
A Division of Grolier Publishing
New York   London   Hong Kong   Sydney
Danbury, Connecticut

RiverFront Books
http://publishing.grolier.com

Library of Congress Cataloging-in-Publication Data
George, Charles, 1949–
    Team skydiving/by Charles and Linda George.
    p. cm.—(Sports alive!)
    Includes bibliographical references (p. 45) and index.
    Summary: Describes the history, equipment, and techniques of the sport of
skydiving and relative work, or team skydiving.
    ISBN 0-7368-0054-9
    1. Skydiving—Juvenile literature. 2. Teamwork (Sports)—Juvenile
literature. [1. Skydiving.] I. George, Linda. II. Title. III. Series.
GV770.G46 1999
797.5'6—dc21
                                                                98-11852
                                                                      CIP
                                                                       AC

Editorial Credits
Mark Drew, editor; Clay Schotzko/Icon Productions, cover designer;
    Sheri Gosewisch, photo researcher

Photo Credits
Aerial Focus/Tom Sanders, 4, 7, 8, 20, 23, 26, 29, 30, 38, 41, 42–43
AP/Wide World Photos, 16
Brent Finley, 34, 37
Corbis-Bettmann, 12
Dembinsky Photo Assoc. Inc./Stuart Williams, 24
FunAir Productions/Michael McGowan, cover, 11, 19
Visual Expressions/Keith Jarrett, 33

Table of Contents

Chapter 1

Skydiving and Team Skydiving

Skydiving is the sport of jumping with a parachute from an airplane. A parachute is a large piece of strong, light cloth. Parachutes allow skydivers to float slowly and safely to the ground. Skydivers store their parachutes in packs. They strap the packs to their backs with harnesses.

Skydivers fall for a period of time before they open their parachutes. This period of time is called free-fall. Experienced skydivers often perform turns and moves during free-fall. Skydivers open their parachutes when they have fallen to a certain altitude. Altitude is the distance of an object above the ground.

Skydivers' parachutes fill with air once opened. A system of strong, thin lines connects parachutes to skydivers' harnesses. Skydivers

A system of strong, thin lines connects parachutes to skydivers' harnesses.

pull on steering toggles to control their speed and direction. Steering toggles are handles connected to the back of a parachute by lines.

Two or more skydivers perform together in team skydiving. Each member of a team falls and moves in relation to the other skydivers. This is why skydivers call team skydiving relative work. The three types of team skydiving are formation skydiving, canopy formation skydiving, and freeflying.

Formation Skydiving

Formation skydiving teams jump, free-fall, and join together while in the air. They make shapes such as doughnuts, stars, and snowflakes. Teams can have 2, 4, 8, 10, 16, or more members.

The altitude from which formation teams jump depends on the number of members. Most teams jump from 12,500 feet (3,810 meters). Small teams jump from as low as 10,000 feet (3,048 meters). Large formation teams sometimes jump from altitudes as high as 20,000 feet (6,096 meters).

The altitude from which formation teams jump affects how much free-fall time they

Formation skydiving teams join together while in the air.

have. They usually have from 30 to 50 seconds to complete their formations. Teams must break away and open their parachutes at the end of their free-fall time.

Canopy Formation Skydiving

Canopy formation skydiving is much different from formation skydiving. Canopy formation skydivers carefully join together as they float

to the ground under their canopies. A canopy is an open parachute and the lines that attach it to a skydiver. Canopy formation skydivers do not free-fall. They open their parachutes immediately after they jump from a plane.

Most canopy formation teams jump from altitudes of 6,000 to 7,000 feet (1,829 to 2,134 meters). Canopy formation skydivers have more time to make formations than formation skydivers do. They have from 90 to 150 seconds to complete their formations and break away.

Freeflying

Freeflying teams have at least two members. In competitions, freeflying teams usually consist of two freeflyers and a camera flyer. The freeflyers perform a series of free-fall moves and tricks called a routine. The camera flyer photographs and videotapes the freeflyers' routine.

Freeflyers perform most of their routines while their bodies are in the vertical position. Vertical means straight up and down. Freeflyers usually fall either headfirst or feetfirst. Freeflyers in the vertical position reach speeds of 180 to 300

Canopy formation skydivers carefully join together as they float to the ground.

miles (322 to 483 kilometers) per hour. Freeflying is one of the fastest sports in the world.

An Extreme Sport

Many people call skydiving an extreme sport because of the sport's level of risk. Team skydiving can be a dangerous sport if team members do not perform correctly. But the risk can be minimized if teams observe all of the necessary safety procedures.

Despite the risk, team skydiving is becoming a popular sport. Today, team skydiving competitions occur around the world. Team skydivers compete with one another on the SkySportif International (SSI) Pro Tour. The SSI Pro Tour holds four competitions each year in different countries. Skydiving teams also compete at the Summer X Games. The X Games is a competition that features many extreme sports.

Team skydiving can be a dangerous sport if team members do not perform correctly.

Chapter 2

The History of Team Skydiving

The history of team skydiving began with the creation of the parachute. Many people believe the Chinese invented the parachute thousands of years ago. The Chinese drew pictures of parachutes that looked like umbrellas. Stiff frames held these parachutes open. No one knows whether the Chinese ever built or tested their parachutes.

Frenchman Jean-Pierre Blanchard invented the first silk parachute in 1785. His parachute did not have a stiff frame to keep it open. No one knows if Blanchard himself ever used his parachute. But some historians think he successfully tested it in 1793.

Most people believe that a Frenchman named Andre-Jacques Garnerin was the first person to successfully use a parachute. In 1797, he

Most people believe that Andre-Jacques Garnerin was the first person to successfully use a parachute.

attached a stiff-framed silk parachute to the basket of a hot-air balloon. The heated air inside the balloon lifted Garnerin to an altitude of about 2,000 feet (610 meters). Garnerin then cut the ropes that attached the basket to the balloon. He floated down and landed safely with the help of the parachute.

Parachute Improvements

In 1887, an American tightrope walker named Tom Baldwin invented a parachute with a harness. Baldwin's harness attached the parachute directly to his body. No one had done this before. Baldwin jumped from a hot-air balloon to test his parachute. His jump was successful.

An American named Charles Broadwick invented a cloth parachute pack in 1901. He placed a folded parachute in the pack. He then laced the pack shut with a length of cord. Broadwick jumped from a hot-air balloon wearing his pack. The pack's cord was attached to the balloon's basket. The cord unraveled as he fell and let out the parachute.

No one is certain who made the first parachute jump from an airplane. Some say that Captain Albert Berry made the first jump in

Georgia "Tiny" Broadwick was the first woman to jump from an airplane.

Missouri in 1912. Others say an American named Grant Morton was the first person to jump from an airplane. He made his jump the same year as Captain Berry. People agree that Georgia "Tiny" Broadwick was the first

woman to jump from an airplane. She made her first jump over Los Angeles in 1913. She later made more than 1,000 successful jumps.

In 1919, American parachutist Leslie Irvin successfully tested a new type of parachute. The parachute had a hand-operated rip cord. Irvin opened his parachute by pulling this rip cord after a brief free-fall. Most people thought the rip cord had to be attached to the plane. They believed that someone free-falling from an airplane would faint before opening the parachute.

The Skydivers

Many people consider Leslie Irvin the inventor of skydiving because of his test jump. Others disagree because Irvin waited only a few seconds before opening his parachute. But he did prove that people could skydive.

Skydiving advanced when parachutists started to experiment with longer free-falls. Steven Budreau was one of the first parachutists to do this. In 1925, he made a jump from an altitude of 7,000 feet (2,134 meters). Budreau free-fell for the first 3,500

Many people consider Leslie Irvin the inventor of skydiving.

feet (1,067 meters). He tried different body positions to control his movements and speed during the fall. Budreau's jump proved that skydivers could control their movements during free-fall. His jump inspired others to experiment with free-fall techniques.

Relative Work

Skydiving was a solo sport for many years. But this changed in 1958 when Lyle Hoffman and James Pearson created relative work. Hoffman and Pearson moved close to one another and passed a baton during free-fall. A baton is a short rod.

Teams of skydivers started to make formations in the early 1960s. Most of these teams had four members. Skydivers attempted larger and more challenging formations as free-fall and relative work techniques improved.

Canopy formation skydiving began as something for formation skydivers to do after they released their parachutes. The sport quickly became popular. Skydivers found that this type of relative work had its own challenges.

The newest team skydiving sport is freeflying. Freeflying started as a solo skydiving

The newest team skydiving sport is freeflying.

sport. Olav Zipser created freeflying in 1991 at the World Freestyle Federation (WFF) Championships in Florida. He performed most of his routine while falling in the vertical position. No one had seen this done before.

In 1992, freeflying became a team skydiving sport. Mike Vail joined Zipser to compete as a team at the WFF Championships in Arizona. Zipser and Vail's performance inspired other skydivers to form freeflying teams.

Chapter 3

Skydiving Skills

Skydivers learn basic solo skydiving skills before they participate in team skydiving. They learn how to remain stable during free-fall. Skydivers learn how to move their bodies so they can change speed and direction. They also learn how to open and control their parachutes.

Skydivers must know how to work with the wind to master basic solo and team skydiving skills. Air pushes hard against skydivers' bodies and parachutes as they fall. This is called wind resistance. Skydivers use wind resistance to change the direction and speed of their falls.

Free-Fall Skills

Skydivers either increase or decrease the amount of wind resistance to change their falling speed

Skydivers learn how to move their bodies so they can change speed and direction during free-fall.

during free-fall. Skydivers slow their falling speed when they flatten out and keep their bodies even with the ground. The wind pushes against more of skydivers' bodies in this position. Skydivers increase their falling speed by shifting into a headfirst dive. This position creates less wind resistance.

Skydivers free-fall in many positions. The basic free-fall position is the box position. Skydivers in this position face the ground. They arch their backs slightly and bend their knees. Their arms are spread and bent at the elbow. Skydivers in the box position reach falling speeds of about 120 miles (193 kilometers) per hour.

Skydivers nearly double their falling speed in the delta position. They straighten their backs and legs to get into this position. Their arms are straight and pointed behind their backs as they dive headfirst toward the ground. Skydivers control the angle and speed of their dives by changing the position of their arms.

Skydivers use the track position to quickly move across large distances. The track position is similar to the delta position. The only difference is that skydivers in the track position have their

The basic free-fall position is the box position.

arms at their sides, bend slightly at the waist and roll their shoulders forward.

Skydivers can perform turns in any of the free-fall positions. They perform turns by moving their arms, shoulders, and legs. Skydivers first look in the direction they want to go. They then lower the shoulder, arm, and leg facing that direction. Skydivers return to their original free-fall positions to stop turns.

Canopy Skills

Skydivers control their speed and direction when under canopy by operating two steering toggles. Skydivers change the shape of their parachutes when they pull on the toggles. This affects the way that air flows around their parachutes.

Skydivers pull on both steering toggles at once to change speed. This is called braking. The distance that skydivers pull their toggles determines how much they slow down.

Skydivers pull the toggles to just above their shoulders to slow down a little. They pull the toggles to their shoulders to slow down more quickly. Skydivers usually pull the toggles to their waists only when they land.

Skydivers turn by pulling down on either toggle. Skydivers pull the right toggle to turn right. They pull the left toggle to turn left. How hard skydivers pull down on the toggles affects the speed of their turns. A slow, even pull results in a smooth turn. A quick, hard pull makes a sharp turn.

Skydivers turn by pulling down on either steering toggle.

Chapter 4

Team Skydiving Techniques

Team skydiving is challenging and takes a great deal of practice. Skydivers must be able to quickly and safely move themselves into and out of formations.

Skydivers learn team techniques after they have mastered solo skydiving. These techniques are different for each team skydiving sport.

Formation Techniques

The way that formation teams jump from airplanes depends on the number of members. All of the members of small formation skydiving teams try to jump from an airplane at the same time. This gives teams more time to create their formations. Larger teams exit airplanes in groups.

Formation skydiving teams try to jump from an airplane at the same time. Larger teams exit airplanes in groups.

The lead skydivers start formations. These skydivers are called the falling base. Falling base skydivers are always in the box position.

Other formation team members join with the falling base. Skydivers use the delta position to quickly reach the falling base if it is far below. They use the track position to move across the sky if the falling base is far away. Skydivers hold the delta or track position until they are about halfway to the formation. They gradually spread their arms and legs out to slow down. This technique is called flaring.

Formation skydivers dock by gripping the arms or legs of other skydivers in a formation. Skydivers are careful to grip other skydivers gently. A rough grip can upset another skydiver's free-fall and destroy the formation.

Formation skydiving teams create many different shapes. Small teams create doughnuts and stars. Large teams create wedges, diamonds, and snowflakes. Teams often try to make as many different formations as possible during free-fall. One four-way team recently made 37 formations in 35 seconds.

Formation skydiving teams create many different shapes.

Teams must break away safely after their formations are complete. They let go of their grips, turn, then move away. Skydivers check to see if others are next to them. They then make sure the sky above them is clear. Skydivers signal other skydivers when they are about to open their parachutes. They do this by crossing their arms over their heads.

Canopy Formation Techniques

Canopy formation teams build most of their formations from the top down. The two team members that dock first are called the base-pin. Each team member glides behind and beneath the base-pin to join it.

Skydivers approach formations at full speed. They pull their toggles to their waists to brake when they draw near the formation. Skydivers must move themselves into position without upsetting the flight of the people above them. The formation could fall apart if the bottom member is bumped and loses control during docking.

Canopy formation skydivers use different docking methods for different formations. To form a stack, each team member sits on the front edge of the parachute below. Members connect by wrapping part of the parachute they are sitting on around their feet. To form a diamond, members grip one of the front corners of the parachute below. Members hook their feet in others' parachute lines to make a plane.

To form a diamond, canopy formation skydivers grip one of the front corners of the parachute below.

Canopy formation skydivers break away from the top down. Team members let go of the parachutes below them. They pull both of their toggles down to brake. Then members turn away and glide to the ground.

Freeflying Techniques

Freeflying is different from formation skydiving in some important ways. Freeflyers perform their routines in vertical falling positions. They usually fall headfirst or feetfirst toward the ground. They sometimes fall in a sitting position.

The basic body position for freeflyers is the Olav frog. This position is named after Olav Zipser. Freeflyers in the Olav frog fall headfirst. They hold their arms away from their sides. Freeflyers keep their legs bent and slightly apart.

Freeflyers make formations during only part of their routines. They also perform various freestyle tricks and moves. Freeflyers perform twists and spins. They also perform wide backward or forward rolls called loops.

Freeflyers perform their routines in vertical falling positions.

Chapter 5

Equipment and Safety

The basic equipment used for skydiving and team skydiving is the same. This equipment includes a parachute, a reserve parachute, and the harness and container system. The container holds the parachutes and is attached to the skydiver's body by the harness. Team skydivers also wear helmets, goggles, a jumpsuit, gloves, and shoes.

Parachutes, Altimeters, and Jumpsuits

The parachute is the most important piece of skydiving equipment. Skydivers have both a main parachute and a reserve parachute. They use their reserve parachutes if their main parachutes do not work properly. Team skydivers' parachutes are ram-air canopies. A ram-air canopy can be shaped like a square or a rectangle.

Ram-air canopies are made up of sections called cells.

Ram-air canopies are made up of sections called cells. Air flows into the cells and inflates the parachute. Once inflated, ram-air parachutes glide like wings. This allows skydivers to control direction and falling speed.

Altimeters are another important piece of skydiving equipment. An altimeter is an instrument that shows the altitude of an object. Skydivers sometimes wear altimeters on their wrists. Others attach altimeters to the chest harness of their parachute packs. Altimeters show skydivers when they are at the proper altitude to open their parachutes.

All team skydivers wear jumpsuits. The type of jumpsuit formation skydivers and freeflyers wear changes stability, free-fall speed, and body control. Jumpsuits are not as important to canopy formation skydivers because they do not free-fall.

Other Equipment

Most team skydivers wear athletic shoes to protect their feet during free-fall and landing. The shoes that team skydivers wear do not have any lacing hooks. Hooks might snag other

An altimeter shows the altitude of an object.

skydivers' parachutes, lines, or jumpsuits
during relative work.

Most team skydivers wear helmets with face
shields. Skydivers may crash into one another
at any point during relative work. Crashes can
be deadly because skydivers fall at such high
speeds. Helmets protect skydivers' heads if
crashes occur in the air.

Students always make practice jumps with instructors.

Team skydivers wear goggles if their helmets do not have face shields. The force of the wind can cause skydivers' eyes to water. This makes it hard for skydivers to see. Goggles protect skydivers' eyes from the wind and keep them from watering. Goggles also protect skydivers' eyes from small flying objects.

Skydivers usually wear gloves to keep their hands warm. The air is much colder at 10,000 feet (3,048 meters) than it is on the ground. Gloves also protect skydivers' hands from flying objects.

Training

Skydivers take many steps to make sure their sport is safe. They pay careful attention to safety while training. Skydivers and skydiving groups create requirements that skydivers must meet before they attempt relative work. Team skydivers plan and practice formations and routines many times before they jump.

People who want to learn to team skydive must first learn how to skydive. They must complete many hours of ground training before going up in an airplane.

Students are ready to make practice jumps after ground training. Students always make practice jumps with instructors. Skydiving students practice their free-fall and canopy skills until they have mastered them. Students interested in team skydiving then begin practicing relative work methods.

Students interested in team skydiving must take more classes. They learn advanced free-fall methods in these classes. Students learn docking procedures. They also learn the correct way to break away from formations. Students then practice these skills in the air with expert team skydivers.

Dirt Dives

Skydiving teams practice formations or routines on the ground before they attempt them in the air. This type of practice is called a dirt dive. Teams practice grips and moves during dirt dives. They make sure that each team member knows what to do and where to go.

Next, skydiving teams practice their formations or routines in the air. Teams often make several practice jumps. Practice jumps often reveal problems that do not show up in dirt dives. Teams discuss these problems, work out solutions, and practice again. Skydiving teams understand that training and practice keep their sport both safe and exciting.

Skydiving teams practice formations on the ground before they attempt them in the air.

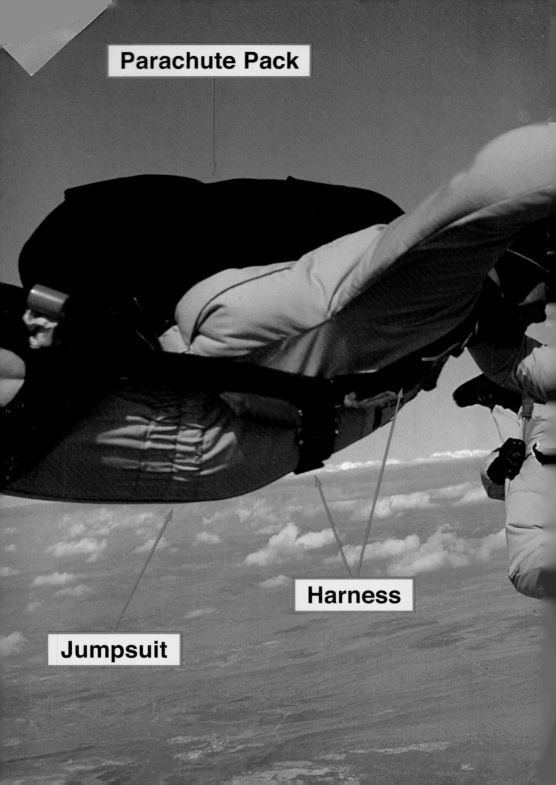

Parachute Pack

Harness

Jumpsuit

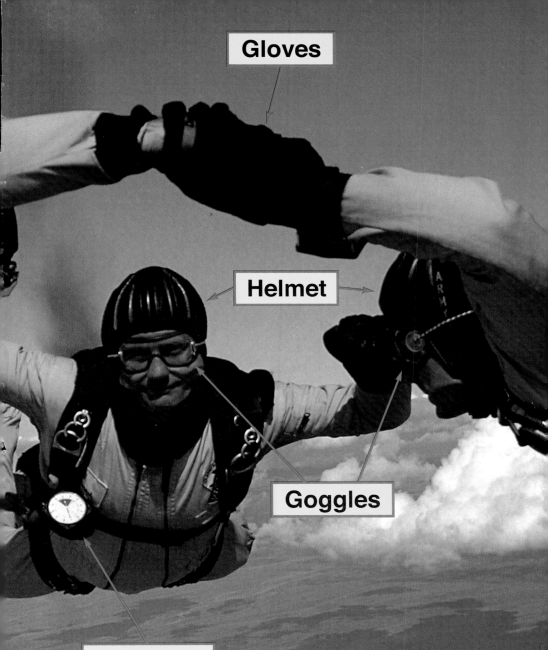

Gloves

Helmet

Goggles

Altimeter

Words to Know

altimeter (al-TIM-uh-tur)—an instrument that indicates the altitude of an object

altitude (AL-ti-tood)—the distance of an object above the ground

base-pin (BAYSS-pin)—the first two skydivers to dock during a canopy formation jump

canopy (KAN-uh-pee)—an open parachute; a canopy consists of the parachute itself and the lines that attach to the parachute.

dirt dives (DURT DIVES)—ground practice for skydiving teams before they attempt formations or routines

falling base (FAWL-ing BAYSS)—the first two skydivers to dock during a formation jump

free-fall (FREE-fall)—the period of time a skydiver falls before opening a parachute

skydiving (SKYE-div-ing)—the sport of jumping with a parachute from an airplane

vertical (VUR-tuh-kuhl)—straight up and down

wind resistance (WIND ri-ZISS-tuhnss)—the force of the air as it pushes against moving objects

To Learn More

Barrett, Norman. *Sky Diving*. Picture Library. New York: Franklin Watts, 1987.

Engle, Eloise. *Parachutes: How They Work*. New York: Putnam and Sons, 1972.

Meeks, Christopher. *Skydiving*. Action Sports. Mankato, Minn.: Capstone Press, 1991.

Tomlinson, Joe. *Extreme Sports: The Illustrated Guide to Maximum Adrenaline Thrills*. New York: Smithmark Publishers, 1996.

Useful Addresses

Canadian Sport Parachuting Association
4185 Dunning Road
RR3
Navan, ON K4B 1J1
Canada

The Parachute Industry Association
1315 Cheyenne Drive
Richardson, TX 75080-3706

United States Parachute Association
1440 Duke Street
Alexandria, VA 22314

Internet Sites

Canadian Sport Parachuting Association
http://www.cspa.ca/

Golden Knights Home Page
http://www.goarmy.com/goldn/goldn.htm

The Parachute Industry Association
http://www.pia.com

SSI Pro Tour: Skysurfing & Freeflying
http://homw1.gte.net/ssipro/

United States Parachute Association
http://www.uspa.org/

Index